Disney

Animated Classics

Studio Fun International
An imprint of Printers Row Publishing Group
A division of Readerlink Distribution Services, LLC
10350 Barnes Canyon Road, Suite 100, San Diego, CA 92121
www.studiofun.com

Printers Row Publishing Group is a division of Readerlink Distribution Services, LLC.
Studio Fun International is a registered trademark of Readerlink Distribution Services, LLC.

All notations of errors or omissions should be addressed to Studio Fun International,
Editorial Department, at the above address.
Special thanks to the Walt Disney Animation Research Library staff for providing the artwork for this book.

ISBN: 978-0-7944-4495-2
Manufactured, printed, and assembled in Dongguan, China.
First printing, October 2019. RRD/10/19
23 22 21 20 19   1 2 3 4 5

This book belongs to

_____

Growing up as a young child in Egypt, I was exposed to a unique and rich culture. My parents would read me stories from *Arabian Nights* before bedtime. "Aladdin" was one of the stories I cherished.

When Disney's *Aladdin* made its way to theaters, I had just turned twelve, and my family had just emigrated from Egypt to Australia. *Aladdin* took me back to a familiar landscape, capturing the essence of the world I once knew. It delivered scene after scene of captivating character animation, and the influence of Arabian architecture was evident. I recognized traits of myself in Aladdin, a young man who wanted nothing more than a better life and over time discovered his own worth. Watching Aladdin and Jasmine fly past the Great Pyramid of Giza on the Magic Carpet, singing "A Whole New World," felt remarkably relatable to the change I was experiencing. It amazed me that storytelling and animation could give me such comfort. That's when I knew what I wanted to do.

It seemed like such an impossible journey back then, but here I was suddenly in 2016, working alongside Ron Clements and John Musker on Disney's *Moana* at the Walt Disney Animation Studios. And Ron and John were the directors of *Aladdin*! The very film that inspired me to pursue a career in animation all those years ago.

Then there's Eric Goldberg, who was the lead animator on the Genie. I had the opportunity to sit with him as he told me stories of Robin Williams, who voiced the Genie. Together, Eric and Mr. Williams brought the character to life. But it was Mr. Williams's eccentric improvisation that was essential, not just to the performance of the animated character, but to the flow and development of the entire story. The Genie, Eric said, was a gift to animators.

Thank you, Ron and John, and Eric, and all the artists and production crew on *Aladdin*. It's because of this film that I found myself part of the next generation of Disney storytellers, pledging to continue the legacy of inspiring future generations to pursue their dreams.

Yasser Hamed
Walt Disney Animation Studios

 n a shimmering city at the edge of a desert, a young man ran

across the rooftops. His name was Aladdin. Behind him ran the royal guards, trying to catch him.

"Stop, thief!" shouted the captain.

"All this for a loaf of bread?" said Aladdin, looking at the loaf in his hands. Then he leaped from the rooftop, swung from a washing line, and crash-landed on the sunbaked ground below.

"There he is!" shouted one of the guards. "You won't get away so easy."

"You think that was easy?" said Aladdin.

The women standing nearby shook with laughter, "Getting into trouble a little early today, aren't you, Aladdin?"

"Trouble?" said Aladdin. "No way. You're only in trouble if you get caught."

But before Aladdin could take another step, the captain of the guards grabbed him. "Gotcha!" he cried.

A moment later, a monkey leaped onto the captain's head and pulled his headpiece over his eyes.

"Perfect timing, Abu, as usual," said Aladdin, grinning. "Come on, let's get out of here."

Together, Aladdin and Abu raced through the narrow streets until they lost sight of the guards.

It was time to enjoy their bread. Aladdin split the loaf, but before he could take a bite, he spied two hungry children watching him with huge, sad eyes. "Here," he said holding out his bread to them. "Go on, take it."

When Aladdin finally arrived home that night, he pulled back his ragged curtain and gazed out across the city. In the distance, he could see the royal palace. "Someday, Abu, things are going to change," he promised. "We'll be rich, live in a palace, and never have any problems at all."

Inside the palace, however, things were not going smoothly. Princess Jasmine's latest suitor was storming out the door.

"Good luck marrying her off!" the suitor told the Sultan as he stalked away.

The Sultan ran to the palace gardens in search of his daughter. She was sitting by a fountain with her pet tiger, Rajah.

"Dearest," he began, "you've got to stop rejecting every suitor who comes to call."

"If I do marry, I want it to be for love," protested the princess. "Please, try to understand. I've never done a thing on my own. I've never had any real friends."

Rajah growled.

"Except you, Rajah," added Jasmine. "I've never even been outside the palace walls."

"But, Jasmine, you're a princess," said her father.

"Then maybe I don't want to be a princess anymore," she replied.

A little while later, the Sultan was pacing inside his throne room.

"It's this suitor business," he told his most trusted advisor, Jafar. "Jasmine refuses to choose a husband. I'm at my wits' end."

"Perhaps I can divine a solution to this thorny problem," offered Jafar. "But it would require the use of the Mystic Blue Diamond."

"Oh, my ring?" asked the Sultan, gazing down at it. "But it's been in the family for years."

"Don't worry," said Jafar, placing his snake-headed staff before the Sultan. "Everything will be fine."

As he spoke, the eyes of the snake glowed red, hypnotizing the Sultan.

"Everything will be fine," repeated the Sultan, his eyes turning the color of the snake's.

"Here, Jafar," said the Sultan as he handed over the ring. Then, with a satisfied grin, Jafar strode from the room.

"Soon, I will be sultan . . ." Jafar said, narrowing his eyes.

The next morning, Princess Jasmine walked down the bustling market streets for the first time. She disguised herself in regular clothes and hid her crown beneath a scarf.

"Pretty lady, buy a pot," called a smiling street seller.

"Sugar dates and figs," cried another.

Aladdin caught sight of Jasmine. He had never seen her before. He watched as she plucked an apple from a stall and handed it to a small child.

"You'd better be able to pay for that!" the fruit seller demanded.

"Pay?" said the princess. "I'm sorry, sir. I don't have any money."

"Thief!" shouted the fruit seller.

At that, Aladdin leaped down in front of the man and shook his hand. "Thank you, kind sir," he said. "I'm so glad you found her."

Aladdin turned to Jasmine. "I've been looking all over for you."

"What are you doing?" she whispered.

"Just play along," Aladdin whispered back.

"You know this girl?" asked the fruit seller.

"Sadly, yes," explained Aladdin. "She is my sister. She's a little crazy. Now come along, Sis," he said, leading her away. "Time to go see the doctor." They were nearly free when Abu dropped the items he had stuffed in his vest while the fruit seller was distracted.

"Come back here, you little thieves!" cried the fruit seller as they fled.

In a secret room deep inside the palace, Jafar inserted the Sultan's ring between two golden snakes' heads. A spark of electric power surged between them into a giant hourglass.

"Part, sands of time," hissed Jafar. "Reveal to me the one who can enter the cave."

At the bottom of the hourglass, there appeared a vision of Aladdin climbing a ladder.

"There he is," gloated Jafar. This was the person who would lead him to the Cave of Wonders, which contained the powerful magic lamp he so desperately desired.

"That's him?" squawked Jafar's parrot, Iago. "That's the clown we've been waiting for?"

"Let's have the guards extend him an invitation to the palace, shall we?" said Jafar.

As Jafar cackled, Aladdin was leaping between rooftops with Jasmine at his side.

"Come on, this way," said Aladdin as they entered a bare room.

"Is this where you live?" asked Jasmine.

"Yep, just me and Abu," Aladdin said. "It's not much, but it's got a great view." He drew back a curtain to reveal the palace, silhouetted against the radiant sky.

"So where are you from?" asked Aladdin as he tossed Jasmine an apple from which Abu was about to take a bite.

"What does it matter?" said Jasmine. "I ran away and I am not going back."

"That's awful," said Aladdin. Then he spied Abu trying to steal Jasmine's apple. "Abu!" he yelled.

Abu let out a stream of squeaks.

"What?" asked Jasmine.

"Um . . . Abu says . . . he wishes there was something he could do to help," said Aladdin, and he leaned toward Jasmine, gazing into her eyes.

"Tell him that's very sweet," Jasmine replied.

Suddenly, there was a shout from the stairs. "Here you are!" someone growled. Three guards walked toward them, blocking the doorway.

"Do you trust me?" asked Aladdin, holding out his hand.

"Yes," said Jasmine, taking it.

"Then jump!" cried Aladdin.

No sooner had Aladdin, Jasmine, and Abu hit the ground than the guards were on them. One grabbed hold of Aladdin.

"Unhand him," Jasmine demanded, throwing back her scarf to reveal her crown, "by order of the princess."

"The princess?" gasped Aladdin.

"I would, Princess," said the guard, "except my orders come from Jafar. You'll have to take it up with him."

"Believe me, I will," said Jasmine as they dragged Aladdin away.

Jasmine raced through the palace until she found Jafar.

"The guards just took a boy from the market, on your orders," she said. "What was his crime?"

"Why, kidnapping the princess, of course," Jafar explained.

"He didn't kidnap me. I ran away."

"Oh dear, well, how frightfully upsetting. Sadly, the boy's sentence has already been carried out."

"What sentence?" Jasmine asked.

"Death," replied Jafar.

She gasped. With nothing more she could do, Jasmine ran from the room in tears.

Unknown to Jasmine, Aladdin lay in chains deep in the palace dungeon.

"I'm a street rat," muttered Aladdin while Abu picked at the locks on Aladdin's chains. "And she's got to marry a prince . . . I'm a fool."

"You're only a fool if you give up, boy," came a voice from the darkness.

Aladdin looked up to see an old man inching toward him.

"Who are you?"

"A lonely prisoner like yourself. But together, perhaps we can be more. There is a cave, boy, a cave of wonders . . . with treasure enough to impress even your princess, I'd wager."

"So why would you share all this wonderful treasure with me?" asked Aladdin.

"I need a young pair of legs and a strong back to go in after it," said the old man. As he spoke, the old man showed Aladdin a secret door. "So, do we have a deal?"

The old man, Aladdin, and Abu crept through a secret passage and across the swirling desert sands. At last, they reached the mouth of a cave made of shadows and sand, shaped like a huge tiger's head.

"Who disturbs my slumber?" growled the tiger head entrance to the Cave of Wonders.

"It is I. Aladdin."

"Proceed. Touch nothing but the lamp," thundered the tiger as it opened its mouth.

"Remember, boy," said the old man, "first fetch me the lamp. And then you shall have your reward."

"Come on, Abu," whispered Aladdin. Together they went down a twisting staircase into the Cave of Wonders. Its rooms were piled high with golden treasure.

Aladdin began to search for the lamp. Behind them, flying silently through the air, was a magic carpet.

"Come on out," said Aladdin gently when he spied the carpet hiding behind a pile of treasure. "We're not gonna hurt you. Maybe you can help us."

"We're trying to find this lamp," Aladdin explained.

The carpet beckoned for them to follow, leading the way through dark caverns to a high stone mound. At its top, in a pool of light, sat a plain old lamp. "This is it?" said Aladdin disbelievingly. "This is what we came all the way down here to—"

He turned as he spoke and saw Abu reaching for a giant, glittering ruby. "No!" cried Aladdin. But Abu already held the ruby in his hands. The cave's walls began to shake.

"You have touched the forbidden treasure. Now you will never again see the light of day!" bellowed the Cave of Wonders.

The cave began to crumble in on itself. Rocks fell like rain, and the cave floor turned to molten lava. Just in time, the Magic Carpet flew to rescue Abu and Aladdin. "Carpet, let's move!" cried Aladdin as a huge wave of lava chased them.

They flew back through the narrow caverns, but as they neared the entrance, a large rock fell on them, flinging Aladdin and Abu against a wall and pinning the carpet to the cave floor.

Aladdin clung to the stone wall. He could see the old man at the entrance of the cave. "Help me out," Aladdin begged.

"First give me the lamp," replied the man.

Aladdin held it up, and the old man grabbed it from him. "At last!" he shouted.

Then he turned on Aladdin, his dagger raised. Abu leaped up to protect Aladdin, but the old man flung them both down into the crumbling cave.

As the Magic Carpet watched them fall, it was able to free itself from the rock and rush to their rescue.

With a final roar, the cave's tiger head entrance disappeared beneath the sand. The old man shed his disguise, revealing himself to be . . . Jafar.

"It's mine," said Jafar, cackling. "It's all mine." But when he reached for the lamp, it was nowhere to be found.

Inside the gloomy cave, Aladdin rose from the carpet in despair. "We're trapped," he sighed. "That two-faced son of a jackal. Well, whoever he was, he's long gone with that lamp."

At that, Abu revealed the lamp from behind his back.

"Why, you hairy little thief," said Aladdin, grinning. He held up the lamp. "It looks like such a beat-up worthless piece of junk." Then he looked closer. "I think there's something written here, but it's hard to make out." He began to rub.

The lamp glowed red. Then fireworks burst from its spout, sparkling and crackling through the air. Out of the fireworks rose a gigantic blue genie.

"Ten thousand years will give you such a crick in the neck. Wow! Wow, does it feel good to be out of there!" the Genie cried. "What's your name?"

"Uh, Aladdin."

"Say, you're a lot smaller than my last master," said the Genie.

"Wait a minute," said Aladdin. "*I'm* your master?"

"That's right!" announced the Genie. "The ever impressive, the long contained, the often imitated but never duplicated . . . genie . . . of . . . the . . . lamp!" Aladdin watched in amazement as the Genie transformed rapidly. "Right here, direct from the lamp. Right here for your wish fulfillment."

"Wish fulfillment?"

"Three wishes, to be exact," replied the Genie. "So what'll it be, Master?"

Aladdin thought for a moment. Then he got an idea. "I don't know, Abu," muttered Aladdin, pretending to walk away. "He probably can't even get us out of this cave."

"Excuse me?" said the Genie. "Are you lookin' at me? Did you rub my lamp? Did you wake me up? Did you bring me here? And all of a sudden you're walking out on me? I don't think so. Not right now. You're getting your wishes, so sit down."

Aladdin and Abu sat on the Magic Carpet with the Genie beside them. "We're . . . out of here!" cried the Genie.

They shot up and out of the cave and, like a comet, streaked across the desert sky, eventually touching down on a sun-kissed oasis.

"Well, how about that?" said the Genie.

"You sure showed me," admitted Aladdin. "Now about my three wishes . . ."

Aladdin turned to the Genie. "What would you wish for?" he asked.

"Freedom," said the Genie.

"You're a prisoner?" asked Aladdin.

"It's all part and parcel of the whole genie gig. Phenomenal cosmic power. Itty-bitty living space," explained the Genie. "The only way I get out of this is if my master wishes me out."

"I'll do it," offered Aladdin. "I'll use my third wish to set you free."

13-29A

"Well, here's hoping," said the Genie, and they shook on it.

"So how 'bout it. What is it you want most?" asked the Genie.

"Well, there's this girl . . ." said Aladdin, sighing.

"I can't make anybody fall in love," said the Genie.

"But she's the princess. To even have a chance, I'd have to be . . . hey, can you make me a prince?"

"Now is that an official wish? Say the magic words."

"Genie, I wish for you to make me a prince," Aladdin said.

The Genie snapped his fingers, and at once, Aladdin was dressed in royal robes. He snapped his fingers again, and Abu transformed into an elephant.

"He's got the outfit," announced the Genie. "He's got the elephant, but we're not through yet. Hang on, kid. We're going to make you a star."

Back at the palace, Jafar hadn't given up his plot to take over the throne. He stood before the Sultan, mesmerizing him with his snake-headed staff. "You will order the princess to marry me," he intoned.

But the Sultan was distracted by the sound of trumpets and drumbeats outside. He raced to the balcony to see a huge procession heading toward the palace, announcing the arrival of Prince Ali Ababwa.

And then Aladdin burst through the palace doors dressed in his prince's robes and swept down from the elephant Abu on the Magic Carpet.

"Your Majesty," said Aladdin, "I have journeyed from afar to seek your daughter's hand."

"Prince Ali Ababwa, of course, I'm delighted to meet you," said the Sultan, shaking Aladdin's hand.

Jasmine entered the room, unnoticed.

"Jasmine will like this one," the Sultan said.

"And I'm pretty sure I'll like Princess Jasmine," replied Aladdin.

"Your Highness, no! I must intercede on Jasmine's behalf. This boy is no different from the others," sneered Jafar. "What makes him think he is worthy of the princess?"

"Your Majesty," protested Aladdin, "just let her meet me."

Jasmine had heard enough. "How dare you?" she called from the doorway. "All of you, standing around deciding my future? I am not a prize to be won." She stormed out of the room.

Later that night, Aladdin stepped onto the Magic Carpet and swept up to Jasmine's balcony.

"It's me. Prince Ali," he announced.

"I do not want to see you," said Princess Jasmine.

But as Jasmine went closer, she thought she recognized him. "Wait . . . do I know you?"

"No," Aladdin said quickly.

"No, I guess not." She sighed and turned to go inside.

Then the Genie appeared as a bee buzzing in Aladdin's ear. "Stop her," said the Genie. "But remember," he added, "beee yourself."

"Yeah, right," replied Aladdin.

Jasmine stopped and turned. "What?"

"Uh, you're right," Aladdin called after her. "You aren't just some prize to be won. You should be free to make your own choice. I'll go now."He stepped off the palace balcony.

"No!" cried Jasmine.

Aladdin rose over the balcony again.

"How . . . are you doing that?"

"It's a magic carpet. You don't want to go for a ride, do you? We could get out of the palace. See the world . . ."

"Is it safe?"

"Sure, do you trust me?" Aladdin asked as he extended his hand.

Jasmine remembered Aladdin's words on the rooftop. "Yes," she replied, and placed her hand in his.

They flew over the city, above the clouds, over winding rivers, and past horses galloping across the desert. At last they came to rest on a rooftop.

"It's all so magical," said Jasmine. "It's a shame Abu had to miss this."

"He doesn't really like flying . . . Oh, no!"

"You are the boy from the market," said Jasmine. "Who are you? Tell me the truth."

"I really am a prince," he lied, too afraid to tell her the truth.

"Good night, my handsome prince," said Jasmine as the Magic Carpet delivered her back on her balcony.

"Sleep well, Princess," said Aladdin. And beneath the moon, they kissed.

For the first time in my life, thought Aladdin, things are starting to go right.

But as soon as Aladdin touched down in the palace garden, he was grabbed by Jafar's men. They took him, chained and bound, and threw him into the sea.

The lamp, hidden in Aladdin's headpiece, fell beside him and rubbed against his hands.

"Come on, Aladdin," cried the Genie, rushing him back to the surface.

Aladdin coughed and spluttered. Then he hugged the Genie in thanks.

In the palace, the Sultan was once more under Jafar's spell. "I have chosen a husband for you," he told Jasmine. "You will wed Jafar."

"Father, I choose Prince Ali," replied Jasmine.

"Prince Ali left," said Jafar.

"Better check your crystal ball again," said Aladdin. Then he noticed Jafar's staff hypnotizing the Sultan. He grabbed it and smashed it on the ground. "Your Highness," he said, "Jafar's been controlling you with this."

"Guards! Arrest Jafar at once!" cried the Sultan.

"This is not done yet, boy," Jafar shouted as he spotted the magic lamp hanging at Aladdin's side. He threw a tiny vial on the ground. A moment later, he disappeared in a cloud of smoke.

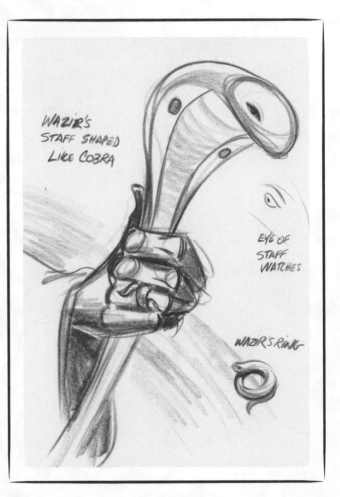

WAZIR'S STAFF SHAPED LIKE COBRA

EYE OF STAFF WATCHES

WAZIR'S RING

That afternoon, under Jafar's orders, Iago flew toward Aladdin's room. He distracted Aladdin and snatched the lamp, then delivered it to Jafar. Jafar rubbed the lamp gleefully. "Genie," he commanded, "I wish to rule on high. As sultan."

At once, a terrible storm gathered above the palace. The Sultan's robes and crown were whisked away from him . . . and onto Jafar.

Next, the Genie lifted the palace and placed it high on a rocky cliff. Aladdin whistled for the Magic Carpet. "Genie, no!" he shouted, flying toward him.

"Sorry, kid," sighed the Genie. "I got a new master now."

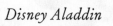
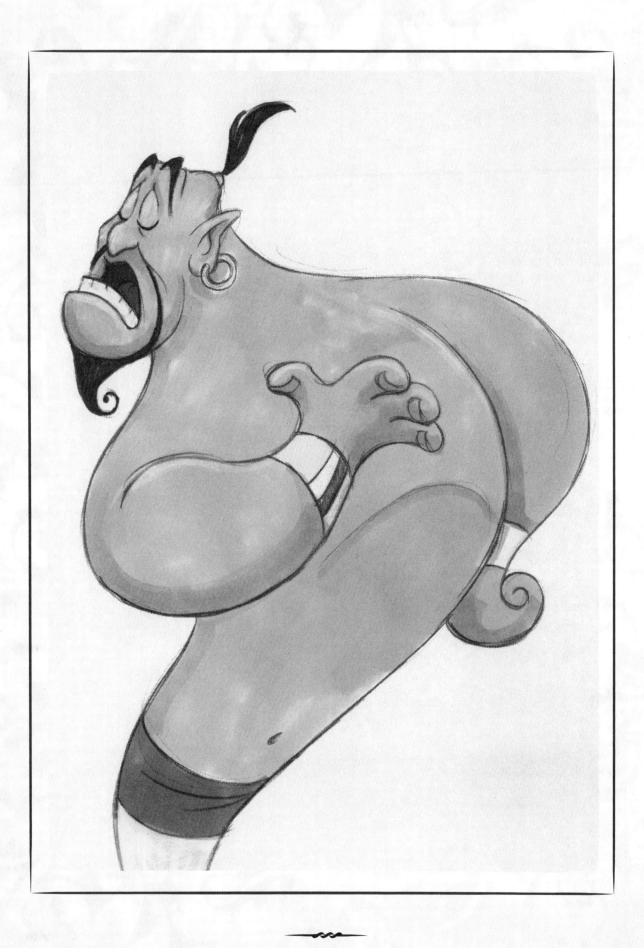

"Genie," Jafar commanded, "my second wish! I wish to be the most powerful sorcerer in the world."

Jafar was lit with a spark from the Genie's outstretched finger. He stood before them, more powerful than ever.

He aimed his staff at Jasmine and her father, forcing them to bow before him. Then he turned to Aladdin, transforming his prince's clothes to his original rags.

"Ali?" Jasmine said.

"Jasmine, I tried to tell you. I just—"

"Genie," said Jafar, "I have decided to make my final wish. I wish for Princess Jasmine to fall desperately in love with me."

Trying to buy some time, Jasmine pretended the Genie had granted Jafar's final wish.

"Jafar," she said, "I never realized how incredibly handsome you are."

But then Jafar spied Aladdin trying to snatch the lamp and knew he had been tricked. At once, he turned on them, trapping Jasmine in an hourglass and surrounding Aladdin with a ring of flames.

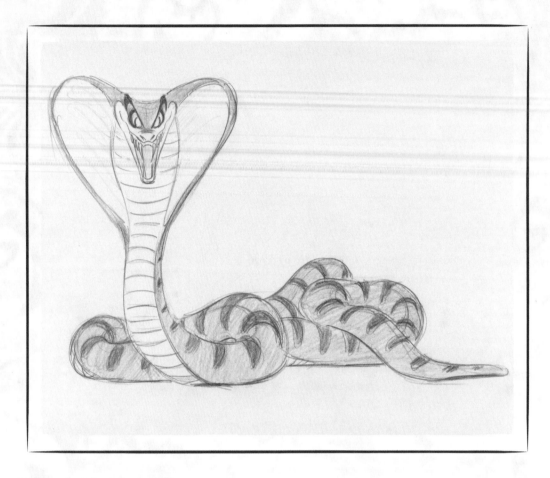

"Are you afraid to fight me yourself, you cowardly snake?" shouted Aladdin.

"A snake, am I? Perhaps you'd like to see how snakelike I can be," Jafar hissed, transforming into a giant cobra and trapping Aladdin in his coils. "You little fool. You thought you could defeat the most powerful being on earth?"

Aladdin paused. Then he got an idea. "The Genie has more power than you'll ever have," he taunted.

"You're right. His power does exceed my own. But not for long. Slave," he commanded the Genie, "I make my third wish. I wish to be an all-powerful genie."

"All right, your wish is my command." And with a zap of his finger, he turned Jafar into a genie. Jafar rose in a red cloud from a gleaming black lamp.

Aladdin raced to free Jasmine from the hourglass as Jafar rose ever higher.

"The universe is mine to command! To control!" Jafar cried.

"Not so fast, Jafar," said Aladdin. "Aren't you forgetting something? You wanted to be a genie? You got it. And everything that goes with it," Aladdin said as he held up the black lamp. Jafar was sucked into it, grabbing his parrot as he went.

"No!" screamed Jafar, but it was too late.

"Phenomenal cosmic powers. Itty-bitty living space," said Aladdin.

In a shower of sparkles, everything returned to normal. Then the Genie sent the black lamp hurtling into the Cave of Wonders.

"Jasmine," said Aladdin, turning to her, "I'm sorry I lied to you about being a prince."

"I know why you did," she replied.

"Well. I guess this is good-bye."

"This isn't fair. I love you," said Jasmine.

"Al, no problem, you've still got one wish left," said the Genie. "Just say the word and you're a prince again."

"But, Genie, what about your freedom?" Aladdin asked. He turned to Jasmine. "I do love you, but I've got to stop pretending to be something I'm not."

"I understand," said Jasmine.

"Genie," said Aladdin, "I wish for your freedom."

There was a burst of light. The cuffs fell from the Genie's wrists. The lamp clattered to the ground.

"I'm free! I'm free at last!" the Genie cheered.

"I'm going to miss you," said Aladdin.

"Me too, Al," the Genie replied. "No matter what anybody says, you'll always be a prince to me."

"That's right!" the Sultan declared. "You've certainly proven your worth as far as I'm concerned. From this day forth, the princess shall marry whomever she deems worthy."

"Him!" Jasmine cried, running into Aladdin's arms. "I choose *you*, Aladdin."

"All of you, come over here," said the Genie, gathering everyone in his arms. "Big group hug!" Then he went swirling into the sky.

"I'm out of here!" he called. "Bye, you two crazy lovebirds."

Aladdin and Jasmine waved good-bye. Then the Magic Carpet swept them away through the night sky, fireworks sparkling above them, as they began their new life together . . .

~≈~

living happily ever after.

The End

~≈~

The Art of Disney's Aladdin

Based on an Arabic folktale, the 1992 release of *Aladdin* was somewhat of a departure from Disney's classic fairy tale film releases. The look of the film took inspiration from Disney's 1940s and 50s animation, contrasting against the realism of the 1991 release *Beauty and the Beast*. The artists also turned to the work of caricaturist Al Hirschfeld, whose flowing, swooping lines are reminiscent of Arabic calligraphy. The animators were inspired by the actors who voiced the characters, using their gestures and facial expressions as reference. This can be seen most vividly in Eric Goldberg's animation of the Genie, voiced by Robin Williams. Throughout this book you can see story sketches, background paintings, concept art and more from the following Disney Studio artists.

Jean Gillmore

Joining Disney in the early 1990s, Jean Gillmore worked as a character designer, eventually specializing in costume design, on some of Disney and Pixar Animation's biggest animated features of the 1990s and 2000s. Gillmore has worked on character design on films including *Aladdin*, *Pocahontas*, *Toy Story*, and *Mulan*. Notably, Gillmore worked on *Frozen* as a visual development artist, helping to create the sumptuous and iconic costumes of the 2013 hit.

Concept art on pages 7, 18, 46, and 50.

Hans Bacher

Hans Bacher, born in Germany, is a well-known and respected animation artist. He began his Disney career in 1987 and has worked as a production designer, visual development artist, storyboard artist, and character designer on films including *Aladdin*, *Beauty and the Beast*, *The Lion King*, *Hercules*, and *Mulan*.

Concept art on pages 8-9, 12, and 34.

Dean Gordon

Dean Gordon worked at the Walt Disney Animation Studios as art director and background supervisor, working on features including *Aladdin*, *Beauty and the Beast*, *The Rescuers Down Under*, and at Disneytoon Studios for *Tarzan 2*. Gordon worked as art director on the Ottorino Respighi's *Pines of Rome* segment for *Fantasia/2000*.

Cel on page 17.

Eric Goldberg

Eric Goldberg joined Disney to work on *Aladdin* and has worked as a supervising animator, writer, and director across many of Disney's other animated features including *Pocahontas*, *The Princess and the Frog*, and more recently *Frozen* and *Moana*. For *Aladdin*, Goldberg was the supervising animator for the Genie. The animation of the Genie was very much inspired by the mannerisms of Robin Williams, the voice actor for the role. Goldberg had the opportunity to study Williams during a stage session, to help flesh out the character animation.

Concept art on pages 15, 41, and 57.

Mark Henn

In 1978, Henn studied in the Walt Disney Character Animation at CalArts and was hired by Walt Disney Studios in 1980. His first big assignment was to animate Mickey Mouse in *Mickey's Christmas Carol*—since then he has worked on dozens of Disney's biggest films, specializing in animating female characters such as Ariel in *The Little Mermaid*, Belle in *Beauty and the Beast*, Jasmine in *Aladdin*, the title character of *Mulan*, Tiana in *The Princess and the Frog*, and Anna in *Frozen*.

Concept art on pages 22, 59, 63, and animation drawing on page 52.

Will Finn

Working as an animator, writer, director, voice actor, and storyboard artist, Will Finn's career in animation has spanned over four decades. For the Walt Disney Studios, Finn has animated many characters including Francis and Georgette in *Oliver & Company*, Sir Grimsby in *The Little Mermaid*, Cogsworth in *Beauty and the Beast*, and Iago in *Aladdin*. He has worked as a writer on *The Hunchback of Notre Dame* and as writer and director on *Home on the Range*. Finn also voiced Hollywood Fish in the 2006 film *Chicken Little*.

Concept art on page 26.

Glen Keane

Glen Keane, one of Disney's most prominent lead character animators, joined the Walt Disney Studios in 1974 and worked at the studios for over 35 years. During his time at Disney, Keane specialized in lead character animation and worked on much-loved characters including Elliott in *Pete's Dragon*, Beast in *Beauty and the Beast*, and the titular characters in *Aladdin*, *Pocahontas*, and *Tarzan*. He subsequently was the supervising animator for John Silver in *Treasure Planet* and served as executive producer, animation supervisor, and directing animator on *Tangled*.

Rough animation drawing on page 27 and concept art on page 29.

———— ❦ ————

Michael Show

Starting at the Walt Disney Animation Studios in the late 1980s, Michael Show has animated some of Disney's most beloved characters and sidekicks including Abu in *Aladdin*, Cogsworth in *Beauty and the Beast*, Timon in *The Lion King*, and Ray in *The Princess and the Frog*.

Animation drawing on page 40.

Alex Kupershmidt

Ukrainian-born Alex Kupershmidt relocated to New York as a young adult and joined the Walt Disney Company's Orlando-based marketing department following graduation. Kupershmidt has worked as animator and supervising animator, bringing to life characters such as the titular character of *Aladdin*, the Hyena Clan in *The Lion King*, Khan and General Li in *Mulan*, and Stitch in *Lilo and Stitch*. Most recently, Kupershmidt has worked on the animation of shorts *Paperman* and *Get a Horse!*.

Concept art on pages 39 and 47.

Francis Glebas

Francis Glebas worked at the Walt Disney Studios as a storyboard artist, director, and writer, contributing to many feature-length animated films and TV series, including *Aladdin*, *The Lion King*, *Hercules*, *Pocahontas*, *Elena of Avalor*, and *Mini Adventures of Winnie the Pooh*. For *Fantasia/2000*, Glebas directed the segment visualizing Sir Edward Elgar's *Pomp and Circumstance* segment.

Concept art on pages 55 and 67.

———— ❦ ————

Doug Krohn

Doug Krohn was an animator at the Walt Disney Studios from 1979 to 2002, where he worked on a number of feature films including *Mickey's Christmas Carol*, *The Little Mermaid*, *Beauty and the Beast*, *Hercules*, *Tarzan*, and *Treasure Planet*. Krohn specialized in character animation and throughout his career at Disney, he helped animate many iconic characters including Belle in *Beauty and the Beast*, Jasmine in *Aladdin*, Jane in *Tarzan*, Milo in *Atlantis: The Lost Empire*, and Jim Hawkins in *Treasure Planet*, as well as the titular characters in *Pocahontas* and *Hercules*. *Animation drawing on page 48.*

Andreas Deja

Polish-born animator Andreas Deja joined the Walt Disney Studios animation department in 1980, and quickly established himself as a supervising animator on some of the most memorable Disney villains. He has animated Gaston in *Beauty and the Beast*, Jafar in *Aladdin*, and Scar in *The Lion King*. Deja doesn't always animate the bad guys. For *The Little Mermaid* Deja animated King Triton, as well as the titular character from *Hercules*, Lilo in *Lilo and Stitch*, and Tigger in the 2011 animated feature *Winnie the Pooh*. In 2015, Deja was named a Disney Legend. *Concept art on pages 56 and 60.*

Sue Nichols

Sue Nichols joined the Walt Disney Animation Studios in the 1980s, first working in the Development Department, generating illustration ideas at a very early stage of an animation's development. For *Aladdin*, Nichols worked on research and development, creating character concept art to inspire animators such as Andreas Deja and others. Nichols went on to work on the visual development for many iconic animated films including *Beauty and the Beast*, *Hercules*, *The Lion King*, and *Mulan*.

Concept art on pages 39 and 47.

Burny Mattinson

Working with the Walt Disney Animation Studios for over 65 years, Burny Mattinson has almost done it all. Beginning with the company in 1953, Burny has been an animator, story artist, writer, director, and producer for over a half century of Disney classics such as *Sleeping Beauty*, *The Jungle Book*, *The Rescuers*, *Mickey's Christmas Carol*, *The Great Mouse Detective*, *The Little Mermaid*, *Aladdin*, *The Lion King*, and *Big Hero 6* among others. His continuing love of the medium of animation and for the simple joys of storytelling are an inspiration for filmmakers and audiences around the world.

Story sketches on pages 14, 19, 20, 44, and 54.

Glossary of Terms

Concept art: drawings, paintings, or sketches prepared in the early stages of a film's development. Concept art is often used to inspire the staging, mood, and atmosphere of scenes.

Story Sketch: shows the action that's happening in a scene, as well as presenting the emotion of the story moment. Story sketches help visualize the film before expensive resources are committed to its production.

Background painting: establishes the color, style and mood of a scene. They're combined with cels for cel set-ups or for the finished scene. The backgrounds also include any of the pages used in the live action storybook that begins and ends the film.

Rough animation drawing: a drawing created very early in the animation process to test an animation.

Animation drawing: an illustration created for the final animation, ready to be traced onto a cel.

Cel: a sheet of clear celluloid, on which animation drawings are traced using ink and painted with color. To create a finished frame of a scene, the cel is photographed against the background painting, which shows through the unpainted areas.

Final frame: Animated films are made up of a series of individual pictures or frames that, when viewed in rapid succession, create the illusion of movement. Individual pictures from these series are called "final frames" and are usually created for publicity or decorative purposes.